Contents

Acknowledgment: Endpaper illustration by James Hodgson

First Edition

© LADYBIRD BOOKS LTD MCMLXXXI

The Red Book of
bedtime stories

Ladybird Books
Loughborough

The Sun and the fish

by Valerie J Appleby
illustrated by Angie Sage

One evening, just as he was setting in the west, the Sun slipped and fell SPLASH! into the sea. The whole world went dark, and the Moon had to come out early to shine in his place.

The Moon *was* cross.

"That Sun gets more and more careless every day," she said, "and now just look at him – blowing bubbles as though it didn't matter! Well, *I* can't get him back again. He's too heavy. The sailors must think of a plan."

"We already have!" said the sailors. "It's quite simple, really. We need a strong rope. Then we'll PULL the Sun from the water, like pulling up an anchor."

They searched everywhere for a strong rope and, at last, they found the very one they were looking for. It was as thick as a tree-trunk, and so heavy it took hundreds of sailors to pick it up.

Using lots of different knots, they tied the huge rope round the middle of the Sun, then to the backs of their great ships. Then the ships pulled and pulled.

"Heave-ho! Heave-ho!" cried the sailors.

Up came the Sun, inch by inch. Then SNAP! The rope gave way! The plan had failed – and the time for morning had come, except of course, there can't be a morning without the Sun. Not that he cared. He was still sitting there blowing bubbles in the sea.

The Moon frowned.

"I suppose I must shine all day as well as all night," she sighed. "It is a nuisance. But I'm sorry for the people below. It isn't their fault."

And looking down, she called out helpfully: "Can't you use a net?"

"Thank you!" cried the people. "The fishermen are making one now. They're going to LIFT the Sun from the water, like catching fish."

All day long, the fishermen worked by moonlight, making the huge net. At last it was finished. It fitted perfectly, but when they lifted it up the Sun was so heavy he fell right through into the water again – SPLASH!

Another day had gone, and the Moon was still shining on her own.

"We must think of another plan," she said wearily. "Perhaps the soldiers can help."

The soldiers thought hard for a few minutes, then they, too, had an idea.

"We've tried pulling, and we've tried lifting," they said, "but they haven't worked. So we're going to BLOW the Sun from the water. It's the only way to get him into the sky again. Men, fetch the gunpowder and put it round the bottom of the Sun."

The Soldiers brought the gunpowder in great barrels, and stacked it carefully round the bottom of the Sun. Then they lit the fuse.

BANG! went the gunpowder.

"Ouch!" cried the Sun, but when they all looked after the smoke had cleared away, he was still there, sitting in the water, but this time he looked very, very sorry for himself.

"I'm tired of being pulled and lifted and blown up out of the water," he grumbled, "and it's no fun any more blowing bubbles. I want to go home."

The people were worried. They had tried everything, but nothing had worked. They couldn't see properly in the moonlight, and they felt cold. Besides this, the flowers wouldn't open, and the corn was beginning to droop. The Moon was beginning to droop, too.

"Oh dear!" she said. "I feel so tired, it wouldn't surprise me if *I* fell into the sea as well," – which was even more worrying.

But there was one little creature that wasn't worried. He was Jonathan Fin, the fish. Plain and brown, no one took the slightest notice of him as he swam about in his muddy little pool. So, when he said, "I've got an idea," everyone stared.

"What, *you*!" cried the people.

"Yes, me," said Jonathan. "I'd like to try."

At last the people agreed. After all, things couldn't be much worse.

So away swam Jonathan, on and on to the sea. There was the Sun, sitting sadly in the water.

"Oh dear," he was saying, 'I want to go home. I do want to go home."

He didn't see Jonathan, for the little fish had dived deep into the water. Backwards and forwards he swam, tickling the Sun on his tummy with his long fins.

"Ho! Ho!" giggled the Sun. "Ha! Ha! He! He!" Jonathan went on tickling.

"HO! HO!" roared the Sun. "HA! HA! HE! HE! I can't bear it! I can't stand it!"

Then WHOOSH! he gave a tremendous heave, and jumped right back into the sky!

The whole world went sunny again, and the Moon sank wearily into bed, but not before she had said, "Thank you," to the little fish. The people said, "Thank you," to the little fish as well.

But Jonathan said nothing — not because he was shy, but because something very remarkable had happened to him. His scales had turned bright orange from being close to the Sun!

"Why! I'm a goldfish now," he cried excitedly — and indeed he was.

From then on he was noticed a lot, and the people put him in a big bowl, where he was very happy indeed.

As for the Sun, he was so pleased to be home and so amused at being tickled, that he's never stopped laughing since.

No wonder he looks so cheerful up there in the sky!

Lewis
the grandfather clock

by Bette L Vickers
illustrated by Brian Price Thomas

Lewis was a very old grandfather clock.

He was staying for the time being in an antique shop, where he stood in the corner just behind the door.

The shopkeeper had bought him very cheaply at an auction sale from amongst a bargain heap.

Everyone could see that his name was Lewis, for it was printed clearly, on his face, together with the date when he had been made.

Lewis did not like the shop very much and hoped that soon someone would take a fancy to him and take him home with them.

The corner where he stood was cold and draughty, and at night Lewis found it difficult to keep warm. The hands on his face would droop to twenty past eight, and this made him look very sad indeed.

But in the daytime, when customers came into the shop, he would put his hands to ten minutes to two and try to look very hard as though he was smiling.

The truth was, you see, Lewis was broken. He couldn't really tell the time at all and that is why no one wanted to buy him.

Then one day, Mr and Mrs Pringle came into the shop. They looked at Lewis and immediately took a fancy to him.

"How much is the grandfather clock?" Mr Pringle asked the shopkeeper.

"He's really cheap," was the reply, "because I'm afraid he's broken, and I don't think he can be mended."

"Oh dear," sighed Mrs Pringle. "What a shame – he's got such a lovely case."

"Well, let's buy him anyway," said her husband. "I like fiddling around with clocks – you never know, I *may* be able to mend it."

And so they bought Lewis.

He was so excited – a home at last. And when he saw the house, it was lovely – so cosy and warm.

The Pringles placed Lewis in the hall near the telephone table, and quite near a central heating radiator.

On the telephone table there was another clock – not nearly as big as Lewis – but this one worked.

He was a very superior clock, and looked down his nose at poor Lewis.

"Hmm, fancy a clock that won't work – whatever did they bring you here for?" he said to Lewis. Lewis was very hurt, but try as he might he just could not work.

One Sunday afternoon Mr Pringle carried Lewis into the kitchen.

"Come on – let's see if I can get you working again," he said.

Piece by piece he took all the parts of Lewis out of his wooden case and laid them on the table.

r the great, grey whale,"
sardine, one day.
hy not?" they all piped up,
'Just do as I say."

it off to play hide and seek
sunken ship,
mmy — the littlest one —
them all the slip.

starboard porthole he swam,
d to hide.
ed and looked and looked —
, Sammy?" they cried.

d Tommy and Mary and Pam,
e and Sue,
ie, Maureen and Rose
— what shall we do?

Carefully he cleaned and oiled everything. And very, very carefully he put them all back again – all except the pendulum and weight.

Then he carried Lewis back into the hall and stood him once again near the radiator. Mr Pringle went back to the kitchen for the pendulum and weight, and gently hung them in place.

"There," he said. "Now let's see what happens."

He took the big brass key and placed it in the keyhole – right in the middle of Lewis – and wound him up.

But still he did not work.

This made the other clock more superior than ever and he was very nasty to poor Lewis.

When the winter came Mr Pringle turned on the central heating during the day. The radiator near Lewis made him feel warm and cosy.

One night it was so cold that Mr Pringle left the heating on when everyone went to bed.

Lewis had just settled down for the night when something happened.

When everyone was fast asleep Lewis began to feel rather peculiar. He thought he recognised the feeling but it certainly had not happened to him for a very long time.

His springs began to whirr and whirr and whirr – his weight dropped and – then – his pendulum began – very slowly – to swing to and fro – to and fro.

And just as Lewis was beginning to wonder what it was all about – guess what happened?

His wheels began to turn – the hands on his face started moving – and with a loud hiccup Lewis started to tick-

tock-tick-tock – and then – a crashing BOING BOING BOING rang through the house.

The noise awoke the Pringles, who came into the hall to see what it was all about. When they saw Lewis was working they became very excited.

"I shall give him some more oil tomorrow and put him to the right time," said Mr Pringle. "That's what's done the job, you know — oil, and being warm."

Lewis was so happy that he almost cried. The other clock stopped being unfriendly and they lived together in the Pringles' hall for many, many, happy years.

Sam

"Don't go ne
Said Mummy
"Why not? W
But she said,

So they all we
In the hull of
But naughty
Went and gav

Out through a
Into the seawe
The others loc
"Where are yo

Then Jimmy a
Billy and Geo
Jonathan, Fran
All cried, "No

"If we go home without our Sam
Mum will be awfully mad.
She told us to make sure he didn't get lost –
If she goes and tells our dad

"We'll all have to stay in this afternoon,
Maybe get sent to bed."
And the little sardines wept sardine tears
As William Henry said –

"What if our Sam gets put in a tin,
With oil – or tomato sauce?
Or made into spread and put in a jar?"
But swimming by, a sea-horse

Called out, "Hey – I've just seen your Sam,
Heading straight for the open sea.
I said, 'Where are you going, you silly sardine?'
But he took no notice of me."

"Thanks, old pal," said the little sardines,
As they dried their sardine tears.
"We'll go and fetch him back at once,
Before our mummy hears."

But at the edge of the open sea
They called for Sam in vain,
So they waited among the seaweed fronds
For Sam to come home again.

And where was Sam? He spoke to a shrimp,
A crab and a lobster, too,
But they'd never seen a great, grey whale –
And they didn't know what they'd do –

If ever they did – they'd be terrified!
But Sam only said, "Huh – huh –
I'm not afraid of a silly old whale –
I'll just swim up and say Boo

"And he'll swim away as fast as he can."
But the crab and the lobster sighed,
"You're heading for trouble, you know, young man."
"You're crazy!" the little shrimp cried.

But Sam just laughed and swam on and on,
Seeing cod and herring and plaice –
All kinds of fish he saw that day,
But of a whale – he found no trace.

"It was just a tale to frighten us,"
He said to himself at last.
"There aren't any great, grey whales in the sea.
Now, I'd better get home, right fast –

"It must be tea-time – I'm hungry, I am."
But which was the way to swim?
Nothing but water all around
And it all looked the same to him.

19

Poor Sammy was lost! He cried and cried –
Then suddenly jumped with fright
When a voice boomed out, "Hello, little man –
I must say you're a strange sight.

"What are you doing – so far from home?"
Between his sobs, Sam cried,
"I came to look for the great, grey whale
But I've had to be satisfied

"With shrimps and lobsters and crabs and things
And now I've lost my way.
I want to go home and see my mum –
I haven't seen her all day."

"Poor little chap," said the deep, kind voice,
"Just you climb on to my back.
You've swum a long way, you must be tired,
I'll have you home in a crack."

So Sammy clung tight and away they went,
Through the blue-green waters deep,
Till at last the seaweed came in sight –
But Sammy had fallen asleep –

And through the seaweed came Jimmy and Sue,
With the others all swimming behind,
They'd waited for Sammy the whole day long,
And now – what did they find?

A huge grey monster at the seaweed's edge!
With shrieks they scattered and fled.
Not one of them saw little Sammy there,
Asleep on the great, grey head.

"That's the worst of being such a great big thing,"
Thought the great, grey whale, with a sigh.
"All the nice little fish are frightened of me
And I wouldn't hurt a fly."

Mummy and Daddy, most concerned,
Heard the tale that the children told,
Of the fearsome monster they'd just seen,
They said, "Be as good as gold –

"Go and hide in the hull of the sunken ship –
Don't make a sound at all –
You'll be safe there from monsters –
    and whales as well –
Just stay there till we call."

Brave as could be, they waited there
Till the monster came in sight –
"It's the great, grey whale," cried Dad, with a gasp,
While poor Mum shook with fright.

"Don't be afraid," said the whale, with a smile,
"But your Sammy had lost his way –
He was looking for me, so I've brought him back –
And please – can I stay and play?"

"Of course you can," said Dad, much relieved,
As the great whale lowered his head
And Mum took the soundly sleeping Sam
And carried him off to bed.

The dragon
that banished the cold

by Mary E Hurst
illustrated by Rosemary Farrell

King Horace of the Land of Glim sat shivering on his throne. "This really is too bad," he muttered to himself crossly. "The middle of winter, snow on the ground, and not one scrap of heat in the land. I'm so cold I can't stop my teeth ch-ch-chattering."

King Horace had no one but himself to blame for this sorry state of affairs, because he had been rude and unkind to Withy the Witch. She wasn't a bad old soul really – she wasn't one of the wicked witches. In fact, she was a great help sometimes with her various spells, but she was getting very shortsighted. One day she had accidentally flown into King Horace's new greenhouse on her broomstick, shattering the glass and spoiling the plants he was growing inside. He had told her crossly to go away and take her mangy black cat with her. He then went on to say that he didn't think much of witches anyway, whatever they were driving – broomsticks, horses, carts or anything else.

Poor old Withy was still very shaken after her accident, and also worried in case her cat and broomstick had been hurt. She had left in a great huff, muttering a curse as she went which spirited away all the matches in the land. Off she went, flying into the East, with thousands and thousands of matches flying after her.

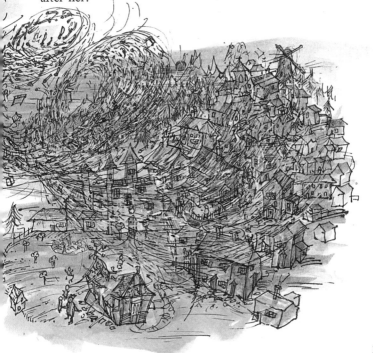

At first it didn't matter very much, because the weather was fine and most houses already had a fire burning in the grate in the kitchen so that people could cook. After a few days however, there was a howling gale which blew right down the chimneys, through doors and windows, and even cracks in the walls. It blew so hard that all the fires went out, and then the problems started.

No one could cook or boil kettles and people were soon fed up with cold food and cold drinks. Then winter struck, bringing frost and snow and casting gloom everywhere. Everyone put on all the clothes they could find and knitted extra woollies, socks and gloves.

King Horace started 'Keep Warm' classes in the mornings, and the people gathered in the huge castle hall to do exercises and try to keep warm. It was no good. The king sent for his court advisers but they could not help. The most important adviser, who had once been a Scout, said he had heard that if two sticks were rubbed together fast enough, sparks would fly and a fire would start. They tried this, but somehow they couldn't make it work, and so the terrible cold continued.

Then one day, when a small boy called John was wandering through the forest looking for fruit, he heard a strange sound. It was rather like a moan, mixed with a sad roar. At first he was frightened and wanted to run, but then he thought that perhaps someone was in trouble. He crept quietly through the bushes following the sound. Suddenly the moans grew very loud indeed, and there in front of him was a huge hole. At the bottom was a green dragon with big tears rolling down his cheeks. Just as John peered over the edge of the hole, the dragon gave an extra loud wail. "Oh, I'll never get out," he wept. "I'm so unhappy."

"C-c-can I help?" stammered John. Although he felt a bit frightened, he also felt sorry for the dragon. He'd never seen one before, but this one certainly seemed quite harmless.

"Who – who said that?" asked the dragon, looking just as frightened as John. "Please let me see you. I'm not a very brave dragon, so please don't hurt me."

The poor animal looked so sad that John lost his own fear and stood up. "Don't worry," he said. "I'm not going to hurt you – but can I help you?"

"Oh yes, please," said the dragon gratefully. "I thought this must be a dragon trap that I'd fallen into, and that when I was found I would be captured and put in a cage."

"Oh no," said John, looking shocked. "We don't do that sort of thing here."

"You see," the dragon went on, "I come from the neighbouring land of Nid, and I got lost in the mountains on the border. I've been wandering around ever since, and," here the dragon started crying again, "I want my mummy."

John was a bit surprised. He had never thought about it before, but obviously dragons must have mothers. "Well, you're quite a young dragon, then," he said.

"Oh yes," replied the creature. "Very young, I'm only 99 years old."

John blinked and wondered how old the dragon's mother could be, as he tried to think how to get the dragon out. Then he had a bright idea. He pulled down long strands of ivy that clung around the tall tree trunks, and set about weaving them together to make a rope.

"Here, catch hold of this and hold tightly," he ordered, throwing the ivy rope over the edge of the hole.

The dragon caught hold of it, and climbed out of the hole with some difficulty.

"Oh thank you, dear friend," he said happily. "Thank you so much."

"My name is John," said the boy.

"I'm known as Nood," said the dragon.

"Nood from the land of Nid," laughed John. Then he saw that the dragon had hurt himself.

"It's my left wing," said Nood. "I think I've cut it – it happened when I fell."

"Come with me," said John, and he helped the dragon back through the wood to the little cottage which was his home.

When John's mother first saw Nood, she was even more surprised than John had been. However, she set about bandaging
his wing.

"I'm sorry the place is so cold," she said, finding it difficult
to make conversation with a dragon. Then she went on to tell
Nood the sad tale that there were no matches in the land of
Glim, and so no fires.

"Perhaps I could help," said Nood brightly. "We dragons
breathe fire, you know, and I would like to do something to
repay your kindness."

John and his mother were overjoyed. They showed Nood the
fireplace, which was all ready and made up with wood.

"Stand back," ordered Nood importantly, then he said in a
whisper to John, "I'm still a bit of a beginner, you know."

With a mighty roar, Nood shot flame from his jaws, and
soon a fire was burning merrily in the fireplace.

Then John had a wonderful idea.

"Nood, would you come with me to the Palace? I know the
king would be most grateful if you could light his fire too."

The dragon agreed, and soon they were in the court of King
Horace. The king beamed from ear to ear, and leapt from his
throne in a most unkingly manner, saying, "Whoopee – let's
build a huge bonfire outside the castle gates, and everyone can
come around and warm themselves."

It was no sooner said than done, and that evening there were
great festivities around the fire, and dancing and singing.

Nood stayed with John until his wing was better and he
was able to fly again. While he stayed in Glim, he visited
everyone's homes and lit fires for them, and so became very
popular indeed.

Eventually, he said goodbye and flew home to his mother in the land of Nid, promising to return often to see John.

That isn't the end of the story, for as Nood flew away, he passed Withy the Witch returning on her broomstick, the matches still dancing gaily after her. She landed at the Palace, saying that she was not happy living anywhere but in the Land of Glim, and King Horace was very pleased to see her back as he had missed her. Life had been rather dull without spells – especially the ones that always went wrong! He apologised for being rude to her, and a week later a banquet was arranged to celebrate Withy's return.

And do you know who were the guests of honour – apart from Withy and the king of course? Why, John, and Nood of the Land of Nid!

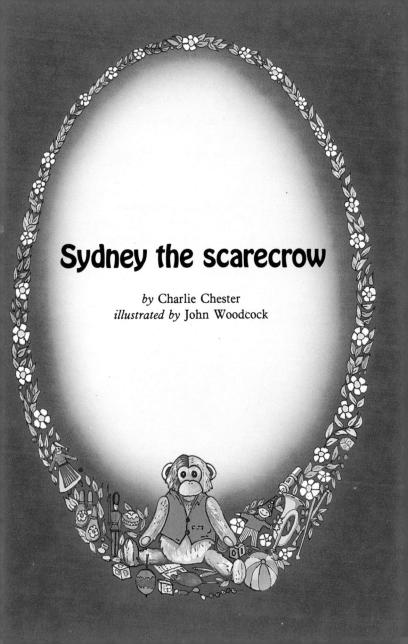

Sydney the scarecrow

by Charlie Chester
illustrated by John Woodcock

One day on Greenfield Farm there was great activity. The farmer was in the fields, working away, planting all his crops . . . it was jolly hard work too, but the farmer didn't mind a bit. As he worked away, he sang a little song:

"I plough the fields, I take the seed,
  Then sow, sow, sow,
  And then the sunshine comes and makes them,
  Grow, grow, grow."

Then the farmer noticed something which made him quite cross . . . he saw all the big black crows fly down to gobble up all the seeds that he had just planted. The birds were pecking away and eating all the seed so quickly that the farmer thought to himself – I must do something about this!

He went to his work shed to get two poles, then nailed them together in a cross. He found some old clothing in the house – an old skirt belonging to his wife, an old brown jacket and a battered old felt hat. Then he put them on the poles, packed and padded them and there was – Sydney the Scarecrow.

Next the farmer placed him in the centre of the field and ripped the clothing a little more so that it would flutter in the breeze. "There you are, my lad," said the farmer. "You flutter away there and frighten off all the birds that steal all my seeds."

Sydney was very proud of himself as he stood there. He didn't mind wearing a lady's skirt at all . . . it fluttered nicely, and he loved his old torn jacket . . . but he hated his hat! He didn't like that a bit. In fact, he longed for a top hat. "If only I could have had a top hat," he thought. "I wouldn't mind how battered it was, as long as it was a top hat . . . a shiny top hat . . ."

As the days went by, all the little animals – the field mice, the rabbits and the hares – used to come and play near him. He liked their company and they became very good friends.

"Don't tell the farmer that we've eaten most of his carrots," they said, and Sydney the Scarecrow told them, "I'm only here to frighten the birds away, so as far as I'm concerned you can help yourself," and they did. They nibbled the lettuce, the carrots, and the beans and had a wonderful time.

One day, Sydney was doing his duty standing guard and fluttering away when suddenly in the distance there was a commotion. There was shouting and little trumpets blaring,

horses galloping, and the noise grew quite frightening. Then Sydney saw something running towards him. As it ran through the stream at the bottom of the field, he saw it was Freddie the Fox — and oh, he was so upset. "Quick, Sydney, what can I do? The hounds and the horses are after me, what can I do?"

"Oh, you poor little fellow," said Sydney. "You can't run any further and whatever you do you'll have to do it quickly — ah, I know — quickly now, hide under my skirt." And as he spoke, the little fox dived underneath Sydney the Scarecrow's skirt. It hid him completely and only just in time, for as he did so, the hounds and the horses all arrived nearby and pulled up, looking for him.

Sydney stood there as if nothing had happened and, to put them off the scent a little more, he began to sing:

"I'm Sydney the Scarecrow,
   Working all the day,
   Fluttering in the balmy breeze,
   To scare the birds away."

"Keep out of sight, little fox," he whispered, "they are still there. If they come any nearer, I'll warn you." The little fox was grateful to Sydney and he trembled with fright as he hid under the skirt. His little heart was pounding with fear.

As Sydney sang, a little breeze started and lifted his hat a little. Then a gust of wind came and blew the hat right off, and it went sailing along the ground towards the huntsmen and their hounds.

The strong wind took the battered hat along so fast that the hounds only got a quick glimpse of something brown rushing past them – and they all thought that it was Freddie the Fox.

Suddenly somebody shouted something . . . "There he goes," cried another . . . and all the hounds started to bark and ran after the hat.

When the hunters were all out of sight, Sydney and the fox stood and laughed till the tears rolled down their faces. "Fancy," said Sydney, "all those horses and men and dogs chasing after my old felt hat," and they laughed again till their sides ached.

"You'd better get going before they come back," Sydney told the fox. The little fox agreed, and after thanking Sydney he dashed off to safety.

Sydney stood deep in thought after the little fox had gone. He was pleased to have lost the old brown hat — but now he had no hat at all.

Then along came the farmer. He looked round for Sydney's old hat, but it had disappeared completely. But what was that at the edge of the field? It was a top hat that one of the huntsmen had lost! The farmer went over and picked it up — and put it on Sydney's head.

It was a beautiful shiny black top hat, and Sydney beamed with joy. Oh, he was proud of himself, and he started to sing:

"I'm Sydney the Scarecrow
And life is simply grand,
I'm the happiest and the smartest
Scarecrow in the land."

Baby Jesus
and the animals

by Ann Ross
illustrated by Hilary Jarvis

The sheep was lost, and all alone in the dark of the night.

"What shall I do?" she said. "I've got nowhere to go."

The sheep looked all around. Then she looked up. Above her in the black sky, twinkling stars were dotted here and there – and everywhere.

Suddenly, far away, the sheep saw a huge star – it was as white as snow, and it shone very brightly.

"I'm going to walk and walk until I reach that star!" said the sheep. And so she did, looking and listening as she went along in the dark of the night.

Now, it was very cold and very windy. But the sheep had lots of long wool all over her body to keep her warm, except on her nose, which was a little bit cold.

After walking for a while the sheep suddenly saw a shadow. She stood as still as a stone and flicked her ears upright. She heard a rustle.

"Who's there?" she asked, afraid.

"Me," said a voice. And a large, skinny dog came out from the bushes. "My master was so poor he could no longer feed me, so I've got nowhere to go."

"Come with me, then," said the sheep. "I'm following that huge star up there."

And the sheep and the dog set off together, looking and listening as they went along in the dark of the night.

Suddenly they heard footsteps. The sheep looked to the left and sniffed the air. The dog looked to the right and sniffed the ground. The footsteps stopped.

"Who's there?" growled the dog.

"Just a tired old donkey," said the voice, wearily. And out of the blackness of the night stepped a donkey with long ears.

"My master kicked me out because I am too old to do any work, and I've nowhere to go," said the donkey.

"Come with us, then," said the sheep. "We're following that huge star up there."

And so the sheep, the dog, and the donkey set off together. They walked for a long, long time, looking and listening as they went along in the dark of the night.

Suddenly they came to where the big star stopped, and in front of them there was a stable. They stood outside.

"I can hear a baby crying," said the sheep, and she peeped inside the stable. The donkey put his head over the top of the sheep's head and he peeped inside. The dog put his head underneath the sheep's head and he too peeped inside.

They saw something sad. There was a baby in a manger, wrapped in a thin sheet, and he was blue with the cold. Sitting beside the manger was a lady and she was shivering as the cold wind blew through the stable. Standing next to the lady was a man, and he was so cold that his beard was shaking.

The sheep, the dog, and the donkey walked into the stable and stood near the baby, the lady and the man to protect them from the cold. Soon their bodies made the air warm and the lady and the man stopped shivering. The baby stopped crying, and smiled and gurgled, and his cheeks went pink.

The animals were very happy. And so were Joseph, Mary and Baby Jesus — they were very glad that the animals had come.

Mary Jane counts to ten

by Olive Phillips
illustrated by Susie Lacombe

Mary Jane wears on her head,
One woollen hat, its colour is red.

On each foot, she wears a shoe –
A pair of shoes – and that means *two*.

On her coat, as you can see,
Mary Jane has buttons *three*.

Mary Jane has dolls to dress.
She has *four* – not more, not less.

On each hand, fingers and thumb
Add up to *five* – try that for a sum!

Six brown eggs are in the box
Made to keep them safe from knocks.

Seven cherries – *seven* stones –
Mary Jane gave seven groans!

Eight birds sing, high in a tree.
Says Mary Jane, "They sing for me!"

In the garden, daisies grow,
Nine of them growing in a row.

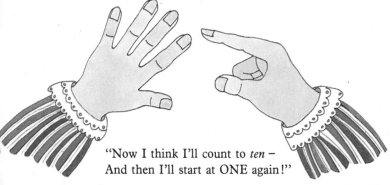

"Now I think I'll count to *ten* –
And then I'll start at ONE again!"